TITLE I

Vincennes Community School Corp.

OTHER YEARLING BOOKS YOU WILL ENJOY:

HAUNTED HOUSE, *Peggy Parish*
HERMIT DAN, *Peggy Parish*
KEY TO THE TREASURE, *Peggy Parish*
PIRATE ISLAND ADVENTURE, *Peggy Parish*
THE GHOSTS OF COUGAR ISLAND, *Peggy Parish*
BEETLES LIGHTLY TOASTED, *Phyllis Reynolds Naylor*
THE AGONY OF ALICE, *Phyllis Reynolds Naylor*
NATE THE GREAT AND THE MISSING KEY, *Marjorie Sharmat*
NATE THE GREAT AND THE LOST LIST, *Marjorie Sharmat*
NATE THE GREAT AND THE BORING BEACH BAG,
Marjorie Sharmat

YEARLING BOOKS are designed especially to entertain and enlighten young people. Patricia Reilly Giff, consultant to this series, received her bachelor's degree from Marymount College and a master's degree in history from St. John's University. She holds a Professional Diploma in Reading and a Doctorate of Humane Letters from Hofstra University. She was a teacher and reading consultant for many years, and is the author of numerous books for young readers.

Clues
in the Woods

by Peggy Parish
illustrated by Paul Frame

A YEARLING BOOK

For Virginia Parish
with love

Published by
Bantam Doubleday Dell Books for Young Readers
a division of
Bantam Doubleday Dell Publishing Group, Inc.
1540 Broadway
New York, New York 10036

ISBN: 0-440-41461-X

Reprinted by arrangement with Macmillan Publishing Co., Inc.

Printed in the United States of America

April 1980

20 19 18

CWO

Contents

1.

Gran's Mystery

"My," said Grandpa, "here it is already August!"

"This summer sure is going fast," said Jed. "Seems as if we just got here and it's almost time to leave."

"But it has been a good one," said Bill. "Figuring out Great-great-grandfather's puzzle and finding the treasure and all."

"Yes," said Liza, Bill's twin sister, "but I almost wish we hadn't found the key to the treasure."

"Why?" asked Jed and Bill in astonishment.

"Because then we could still have the fun of looking for it," said Liza. "Remember how we used to talk about it every summer before we came here?"

"Well," said Grandpa, "I wouldn't worry about it. Maybe by next summer Gran and I can dig up another mystery for you."

"Next summer, indeed," said Gran, coming out on the porch just then. "If it's a mystery you're after, it won't have to wait until next summer. Nor will we have to dig for it."

Grandpa and the three children looked at Gran expectantly. But she didn't say any more. She walked over to her rocking chair. And Gran settled down with her knitting.

"Gran, do hurry up and tell us!" said Liza. "What is your mystery?"

"Disappearing garbage," said Gran.

"Disappearing garbage!" said Jed. "Why would anyone take that?"

"Ah, Gran, you're just teasing us," said Bill.

"Let me tell you the whole story," said Gran. "You know the McNellis family down the road. They are pretty hard put to make ends meet. Well, the little girls found a family of kittens and wanted to keep them. But there just weren't enough table scraps at their house to feed them properly. So they asked me if I would save some scraps for them. They're such dear children that of course I said I would. I've been putting the supper scraps in a plastic bag and sitting them on top of the garbage can each night. Then yesterday morning, my eye just happened to catch a glimpse of the girls leaving empty-handed. I called to them to find out why. They said they thought I had forgotten and didn't want to bother me. I wasn't too concerned about it. Any stray dog might have picked the bag up. But I told the girls I would leave it inside the can after that. Well, they came to me this morning to say the bag was gone again."

"Gee, Gran," said Bill, "maybe it was raccoons."

"No, no," said Grandpa. "Raccoons make such a clatter and leave such a mess, you know when they've been there."

"Nor would a raccoon put the cover back on the garbage can," said Gran.

"Do you think maybe it was a tramp?" asked Jed.

"I doubt it," said Grandpa. "I haven't seen a tramp around here in years."

"And a tramp would be more likely to ask for something to eat," said Gran.

"Gosh, Gran," said Liza, "you really do have a mystery!"

"Yes, the disappearing kitten scraps," said Bill. "But how will we ever find out what's happening to them."

"Maybe we could hide under the house tonight," said Jed.

"Indeed you won't," said Gran. "I told

5

the girls just to knock on the door in the morning. I'll keep the scraps inside."

"Gran!" said Bill. "You can't do that! How can we solve the mystery if we don't know whether the mysterious thief is still around?"

"And we've got to leave those scraps for bait," said Jed.

"But the poor kittens will starve if their scraps keep disappearing," said Liza. "I think Gran is right."

"Oh, pooh!" said Bill. "She doesn't have to leave all of the scraps inside. How much can a few little kittens eat anyway?"

"I'll have to go along with the boys on that," said Grandpa. "Maybe you could just put out a few scraps."

"Well, it's three against two, Liza. We'll just have to save the most kittenish scraps and put the rest out," said Gran. "But you children may not hide under the house or anywhere else outside. You'll have to find some other way to solve this."

"All right," said Jed, "we promise."

"What I think we need around here is a dog," said Grandpa. "Then this kind of thing wouldn't happen."

"Oh, yes," said Liza, "do Grandpa, let's get a puppy. Mr. Sanders has some. He said we would be welcome to one."

"That's up to your Gran," said Grandpa. "Mr. Sanders told me yesterday his pups are big enough to make it on their own if we do want one."

"What good would a little puppy be?" asked Gran. "I thought you said a dog. I declare I wouldn't mind having a dog around again."

"But, Gran," said Liza, "puppies grow very quickly. Even when they're little they bark. Please, Gran."

"Yes, Gran," said Jed, "if you get one while we're here, we could take care of it for you."

"I give up!" said Gran. "Go ahead and get the puppy."

2.

Black Jelly Bean

"Come on, Grandpa," said Bill. "Let's go quickly before she has a chance to change her mind."

"I'm ready," said Grandpa. "Pile in the car."

The children didn't have to be told twice. Soon Grandpa was driving down the road to the Sanders' house.

The Sanders didn't live far away. In just a few minutes Grandpa was turning into the lane that led to the house. As soon as the car stopped, the children jumped out.

"Hi, big children," called a small boy.

"Hi, Timothy," Liza called back.

"Did you come to play with me?" asked Timothy.

"We came to get a puppy," said Liza.

"A puppy!" said Timothy. "I'll show you."

Timothy started toward the barn. Liza, Jed, and Bill followed him. Grandpa turned toward the house.

Just then the door opened and Mr. Sanders called, "Hi, there. Did someone say something about coming for a puppy?"

"Indeed we did," said Grandpa. "Everybody agrees a puppy is a good idea."

"Timothy seems to have everything pretty well in hand. Would you like to see them, too?" asked Mr. Sanders.

"Yes," said Grandpa. "I always did have a soft spot for young pups. I'm glad the children talked Gran into getting one."

By that time the children had reached the barn. As soon as Liza saw the pups she dropped to her knees and squealed.

"Oh, you darling things! I want all of you."

"No!" said Timothy. "Daddy said I

could keep one. And I want this one."

Timothy picked up a fluffy white pup with black spots. He held it close. "And you can't have it," he added.

"Ah, Timothy, Liza's just kidding," said Jed. "Gran would have a fit if we came home with five pups."

Suddenly a sixth puppy popped around the corner and wiggled all over.

"Hey, look at that one," said Jed.

"He looks like a wiggling black jelly bean," said Bill.

"Jelly Bean!" said Liza. "Oh, Jelly Bean is the puppy I want. Grandpa, look at him!"

Grandpa was chuckling away.

"He sure is a lively little fellow," he said. "But you had better ask Mr. Sanders which ones you can choose from. He may have other plans for some of these pups."

"Oh, Mr. Sanders," said Liza, "is Jelly Bean one of the pups we can choose?"

"Certainly," said Mr. Sanders. "The only pup that's spoken for is Timothy's Butterball, and I think he made that clear."

"Hurray!" said Liza. She picked Jelly Bean up and hugged him to her.

"Well, that's settled," said Bill. "Let's go home and show Gran."

"You children certainly are forgetting your manners today," said Grandpa. "Isn't there something you need to do before you go?"

The children all looked puzzled. Mr.

Sanders laughed. "That's what excitement does. That's enough of a thank you for me. I know Jelly Bean will be well taken care of."

"Oh!" said Liza, Bill, and Jed all at once.

"We're sorry Mr. Sanders!" said Liza. "Thank you, thank you, thank you!"

The three children climbed into the back seat of the car. There was not the usual fuss as to who would sit in front. Everybody wanted to sit next to the puppy.

Grandpa had just started the engine when Mr. Sanders called, "Oh, wait a minute. There's something I forgot to give you."

Mr. Sanders went into the house and came back with a large paper bag.

"This is the food I've been giving the pups. I think you had better keep Jelly Bean on it for a week or two. Just mix it with a little milk," said Mr. Sanders.

"Now that is nice of you," said Grandpa. "Not a one of us thought to ask you what to give the little fellow."

On the way home Jelly Bean wiggled happily from one child to another. He seemed to be as contented with the children as they were with him.

Gran was still on the porch knitting when they reached home.

"Back already!" she called. "I was sure it would take all afternoon to choose a puppy."

"Oh, no, Gran," said Liza. "We knew we wanted Jelly Bean as soon as we saw him."

"Jelly Bean! I've never heard that name for a puppy," said Gran.

"It was Bill's idea," said Jed.

"When we first saw him Bill said he looked just like a wiggling black jelly bean," said Liza.

Gran laughed as she said, "Well, he does wiggle. That's for sure."

"Oh, Gran," said Liza, "may I put his bed right next to mine?"

"You may not!" said Gran. "Puppies belong outside. This one is used to it. I don't want him in the house at all."

"Gran!" said Liza, "you don't really mean that, do you?"

"I do indeed," said Gran. "I like dogs, but not in the house."

"Besides that, Liza," said Jed, "remember, we got him for a watch dog."

"Yeah," said Bill. "A watch dog to let us know if anybody is around who shouldn't be. Not a watch dog to watch you sleep."

"Funny, ha, ha," said Liza.

But Liza did not argue with Gran. Gran had that look on her face that said she wasn't going to change her mind.

"You can make him a nice bed on the back porch," said Gran.

So Liza had to content herself with that.

The children played with the puppy for the rest of the afternoon.

"Oh, my," said Gran, "it's time to fix supper."

"I'll fix Jelly Bean's supper," said Liza. "Grandpa, where is the dog food?"

"In the car," said Grandpa.

Liza ran and got the dog food. Then she followed Gran into the kitchen.

"What can I feed him in?" asked Liza.

"Now just a minute," said Gran. "If I'm not mistaken, there's a bowl for food and another for water on that top shelf. I knew someday we would have another dog. I saved them after Terrance died."

"I remember Terrance," said Liza. "What happened to him?"

"He died of plain old age," said Gran. "I guess I was so fond of him I wasn't anxious to get another dog. I don't think I'll ever like another as much."

"You wait," said Liza. "You're going to just love Jelly Bean."

Liza mixed the dog food with milk and went out on the back porch.

"Bill, Jed," she called, "bring Jelly Bean. His supper is ready."

The boys brought the puppy. As soon as Jelly Bean saw the bowl of food he wiggled out of Jed's arms. And he wiggled the whole time he was eating.

"If he doesn't stop wiggling so much, he's going to wiggle himself in half," said Bill.

Gran called the children in to supper. Jelly Bean wasn't happy to be left alone. He cried outside the door.

"Oh, Gran," called Liza, "please can't we bring him in?"

"No," said Gran. "He'll have to get used to staying alone sometime."

"Maybe he's sleepy," said Jed. "After all he is just a baby."

"May I be excused to put him in his bed?" asked Liza.

"That's a good idea," said Gran.

Liza went out and put Jelly Bean in his box. He tumbled around in the rags she had put in it.

Liza came back to the table. For a little while Jelly Bean was quiet. Then the crying started again.

"I'm afraid he's going to cry all night," said Liza, "and I just can't stand to hear him cry."

"Now wait a minute," said Grandpa.

"What was it I read about that? Oh, yes, a clock! If you put a clock in the box with a puppy it won't cry. Don't we have an old alarm clock around, Gran?"

"Yes," said Gran, "and I know just where it is."

Gran went to the cabinet and got down the clock. She handed it to Grandpa. He wound it.

"There, Liza," he said, "put that in the box with Jelly Bean for company."

Liza looked doubtful about the whole thing. But she took the clock and carried it to the back porch. When Jelly Bean saw her he stopped crying and started wiggling. Liza put the clock in the box and patted him.

Liza walked away and Jelly Bean started to cry. But suddenly he stopped. Liza went on inside.

"Gee, Grandpa," she said, "I believe your idea is going to work."

3.
Squabbling Twins

When supper was finished, Gran said, "My, I am tired tonight."

"You go and sit down," said Liza. "We can clear the table and do the dishes."

"I think I'll just let you do that," said Gran. "Don't forget to save the best scraps for the kittens."

"Don't worry, Gran," said Liza.

Gran and Grandpa went to sit on the front porch. Liza began to scrape the plates. She put all the scraps into one plastic bag.

"Hey, Liza," said Bill, "some of those scraps should go into another bag for the trap."

But Liza went right on with what she was doing. Then she buttered two pieces of bread. She put the bread, a pork chop, and some cookies into a second plastic bag.

"Have you gone nuts or something?" asked Bill.

"If somebody's hungry," said Liza, "I think they should have some real food."

"But suppose it's a fugitive? Suppose it's someone who has done something really bad?" asked Bill.

"I don't care," said Liza. "They still deserve to eat."

"Okay, okay," said Bill. "Here, I'll take that out."

"All right," said Liza and handed him the bag.

"Be quiet about it," said Jed. "Remember Jelly Bean is asleep."

"I know, I know," said Bill. He was very careful not to let the door slam.

When Bill came back in, Liza had begun to wash the dishes. Jed was drying them.

"Hey, we better make some plans," said Bill.

"Plans for what?" asked Liza.

"Don't be so stupid!" said Bill.

"I'm not stupid!" said Liza. "I just don't know what we've got to plan anything about."

"Ahhh girls!" said Bill.

"He means about solving the mystery of the disappearing kitten scraps," said Jed.

"Oh, that!" said Liza.

"Oh that, huh!" said Bill. "Well, if you're not interested, Jed and I can solve it. Hurry up, Jed. We won't even let Miss 'Oh That' listen to the plans."

"You will too!" screamed Liza. She picked up a handful of soap suds and threw them in Bill's face.

"Why you . . ." yelled Bill. He picked

up a wet plate and drew his arm back.

"Don't you throw that plate at me!" shouted Liza.

"Bill! Are you out of your mind?" said Jed.

But Bill's cheeks puffed out. His face grew red. He glared at Liza. And Liza glared right back at him. Then Bill's arm slowly lowered. He put down the plate, but he continued to glare angrily at Liza.

"All right, if you two want to just fight, go ahead," said Jed. "I'll make my own plans. And I won't need help from either one of you."

That stopped both Liza and Bill. Jed was the best planner of the three. They knew he meant what he said.

"Oh, all right," mumbled Bill.

"Now come on," said Jed. "Grab a dish towel, Bill. Let's get through here."

With all three of them working, it didn't take long to finish cleaning up the kitchen.

4.

Jed's Plan

"Let's go upstairs to make our plans," said Bill. "It's more private there."

"We better go out on the porch for a few minutes," said Jed. "Gran and Grandpa will know something is up if we don't."

"Oh bother!" said Liza. "But I guess you're right."

Gran and Grandpa were sitting quietly on the porch.

"All through?" asked Gran.

"Yes," said Liza.

"Aren't the stars pretty tonight," said Gran.

"Gee, it looks as if there are millions of them," said Jed.

"Anybody want to go upstairs and play a game?" asked Bill.

Liza was silent.

"Oh, all right," said Jed, "I'll play."

"Well, don't force yourself," said Bill.

"You all run along," said Gran. "Grandpa and I will enjoy the stars a bit longer."

"Aren't you coming, Liza?" asked Bill.

"I guess so," said Liza.

Going up the stairs Bill asked, "What was that all about? It sounded as if you didn't want to go."

Jed grinned and said, "That's just the way I wanted it to sound. Now nobody will suspect us of being up to anything. And I have a plan."

"You do?" said Liza. "When did you think of it?"

"I've been figuring it out all day," said Jed.

"Okay, hurry up," said Bill. He pushed them into Liza's room.

25

"Stop pushing me!" said Liza.

"Oh, don't be so touchy," said Bill. "What's wrong with you anyway?"

"Wrong with me! You started it," said Liza.

"I did not!" said Bill.

"You did too," said Liza.

"Did not!" said Bill.

"That does it!" said Jed. "You both make me sick!"

Jed marched out of the room and slammed the door.

Bill and Liza looked at each other.

"Oh, phooey!" said Bill. "We don't need him."

"But he had the plan," said Liza.

Bill thought this over. He held out his hand and said, "Truce?"

"Truce," said Liza, taking Bill's hand.

Bill and Liza went down to Jed's room.

"Jed, we're sorry," said Liza.

"Yeah, sorry old boy," mumbled Bill.

"Now what's that plan of yours? Come on, spill it."

"Well, okay," said Jed. "We are going to wait until Gran and Grandpa go to bed. Then we will hide out and see who is taking the kitten scraps."

"But Gran said we could not go outside," said Liza.

"Who said anything about going outside," said Jed. "I looked the situation over. We can see the garbage can from the dining room window. You know, that one that goes out at an angle."

"Hey, that's neat!" said Bill, "I never thought about that window."

"We'll get ready for bed the same as usual," said Jed. "Then when Gran and Grandpa go to sleep we'll sneak downstairs."

"Won't we need a flashlight?" asked Liza.

"Nope, no lights," said Jed. "It's not

that dark tonight. We can feel our way down."

"I wish Gran and Grandpa would hurry up and get sleepy," said Bill. "That kitten scrap taker might come before we can get there."

"I doubt that," said Jed. "But why don't we go down and start talking about getting sleepy. Maybe that will make them sleepy, too."

"Let's go," said Liza and started to run out of the room.

"Whoa there!" said Bill. "You've got to act sleepy."

"But if I act sleepy, it might work on me," said Liza.

"We'll take care of that," said Bill. He grinned at Liza and reached out to pull her hair.

"Now stop that!" said Liza. "I think I'll manage without that kind of help."

As the children were going downstairs,

the front door opened. Gran and Grandpa walked into the house.

"Oh," said Gran, "I thought you three were in for the night. Grandpa and I were just coming up to bed."

"We just wanted to say, 'good night,'" said Liza.

"We did?" said Bill. But before he could say more Jed poked him.

The children started back upstairs. Gran and Grandpa turned out the downstairs lights.

"Boy, you almost goofed that up!" said Jed.

"I sure did. All I was thinking about was ways to get them sleepy," said Bill. "I wasn't expecting them to be sleepy already."

"All right," said Jed. "Now get ready for bed and turn out the lights. Then when Grandpa starts snoring, we'll know it's safe to go down. Bill and I will stop by for you, Liza."

"All right," said Liza. She undressed and brushed her teeth. Then she got into bed and turned out the light.

5.

The Big Failure

Liza turned one way and then the other. She wasn't the least bit sleepy. But it seemed as if the boys would never come. The minutes just dragged by.

Finally she heard a whispered, "Pssst, Liza."

"Coming," Liza whispered back. She slipped out of bed and joined the boys in the hall.

"Quiet now," said Jed. "And for gosh sakes don't trip or anything."

Slowly the children felt their way down the stairs and into the dining room.

"We made it!" said Bill.

"Not so loud," said Jed. "It's not just Gran and Grandpa who mustn't hear us."

"Sorry," said Bill.

The three children stationed themselves in front of the window. The night was clear. The sky filled with stars made it seem almost like daylight. A cricket chirped now and then or a breeze rippled through the leaves. But for the most part, everything was still. The children kept their eyes glued to the garbage can, waiting for something to happen. But nothing did.

"Gee," whispered Liza, "I can't sit still much longer. I'm getting sleepy."

Bill began to slip away.

"Where are you going?" whispered Jed.

"To the kitchen," Bill whispered back. "I'm hungry."

"Look!" Liza pulled Jed's arm. "I think I saw something move."

"Where? Where?" said Bill. "Let me see."

Bill rushed in, pushing Jed and Liza aside. Liza lost her balance. She fell against a floor lamp. And over it went with a big crash.

"Now look what you did, you stupid thing!" groaned Bill.

"I did?" said Liza crying. "You pushed me!"

Suddenly the lights went on upstairs.

"What is it? Who is down there?" called Grandpa.

"It's only us," said Bill.

Grandpa came down the stairs with Gran right behind him.

"What was that crash? Why are you children down here with no lights on?" he asked.

Then Gran saw the lamp.

"Oh, no!" she said. "My lamp! My favorite lamp!"

"We're sorry, Gran," said Jed.

Grandpa picked up the lamp.

"Not too much damage done," he said. "I'm sure it can be repaired. But you children have some explaining to do."

"We were trying to solve the mystery," said Liza. "We can see the garbage can from here."

"We were trying to see how the kitten scraps disappear," said Bill.

"I thought I saw something move," said

Liza, still crying a little, "and then Bill pushed me, and I tripped on the lamp."

"Yeah, yeah," said Bill. "It's always my fault."

"Well, this time it sure was," said Jed. "You pushed us both aside and tried to hog all the space. Now we'll never find out anything."

Bill looked unhappy.

"I'm—I'm sorry," he mumbled, "I guess I did get too excited."

"We'll pay for getting the lamp repaired," said Jed.

"I'm not worried about the money," said Gran. "I just hope it can be repaired. I do wish you children wouldn't do things like this."

The children said no more. Gran was very cross with them. And they knew Grandpa wasn't pleased with what had happened either. Slowly they went back upstairs. Without a word each of them went to his own bed.

6.
Mystery Added to Mystery

In spite of their late night the children were up at the usual time the next morning. They raced downstairs with one thought in mind. Were the kitten scraps gone again?

"Good morning, Gran," called Liza as they went through the kitchen.

Jed beat the others to the garbage can and lifted the lid.

"Gone again!" he said.

"And we were so close to finding out who it was," said Liza.

"No use worrying about that now," said Jed. "We'll have to think of some other way to find out."

"Breakfast, children," called Gran.

They went into the kitchen. Gran was still cross about the lamp. Nobody said much to her. But suddenly Liza jumped up from the table.

"Jelly Bean!" she said, "I forgot all about him."

Liza ran out to the back porch. She could hear the clock ticking merrily. Liza looked into the box expecting to be greeted by a wiggling puppy — or at least a sleeping one. But there was no puppy! Only the rags and the clock were in the box.

"He's gone! Jelly Bean is gone!" shouted Liza.

Jed and Bill ran out on the porch. They looked in the box. But they, too, saw only the rags and the clock.

"Gran!" called Liza, "Jelly Bean is gone!"

Gran was at the door. She said, "Maybe he's with Grandpa."

"Maybe who's with Grandpa?" asked

Grandpa coming up to them just then.

"Jelly Bean. Grandpa, have you seen Jelly Bean?" asked Liza.

"No," said Grandpa, "I haven't seen him this morning."

"You haven't?" said Liza. "Then where can he be?"

"Maybe he decided to do some exploring on his own," said Grandpa. "Come on, I'll help you look for him."

They all started out in different directions.

"Here, Jelly Bean, come here old boy," called Bill.

All over the yard they looked and called. But no black puppy came to them.

A little later Grandpa looked toward the road. Then he started walking in that direction. The children saw him, and without a word they followed.

Finally Liza said, "Grandpa! You don't think a car hit him, do you?"

"I don't want to think that," said Grandpa. "But you never can tell. He may have seen someone on the road and followed him."

Grandpa started looking in the bushes along the side of the road. The children joined in the search. Everyone dreaded what they might find, but they knew they had to look. Up and down the road they went. But there was no black puppy.

"That makes me feel better," said

Grandpa. "He may have followed someone without their knowing it. I expect
they will call the neighbors to find out
who is missing a puppy."

"Then let's get back to the house," said
Liza. "The telephone might be ringing
now."

"Well, I'm sure Gran knows how to answer it," said Grandpa with a chuckle.

"Grandpa!" said Liza. "You know what
I mean."

But when they reached the house there
had been no telephone call.

All morning long the children hung
around the house. No one was able to get
interested in anything. They stayed out of
Gran's way. All three felt badly about the
lamp.

Grandpa was away most of the morning
on business. He didn't get back until
lunchtime.

"Come, children," called Gran. "We're
ready for lunch."

There was still no smile on Gran's face. But neither were there smiles on the children's faces. There had been no word about Jelly Bean.

"I took the lamp in to Mr. Lemon," said Grandpa. "He said there would be no trouble about repairing it."

"I hope he's right," said Gran.

The children didn't say anything. They could not understand how Gran could be that upset about a lamp.

"Oh, by the way," said Gran, "who brought Liza's red sweater in off the clothesline?"

"My red sweater?" asked Liza.

"Yes," said Gran. "Remember, you spilled hot chocolate on it? I washed it yesterday and forgot to bring it in. When I went out to get it a bit ago, it wasn't there. One of you did bring it in, didn't you?"

Gran looked around the table. Grandpa, Jed, Bill, and Liza shook their heads.

"Then what could have happened to it?" asked Gran.

"Are you sure it didn't just get blown off the line?" asked Grandpa.

"If it did, why wasn't it on the ground?" asked Gran. "I looked all around. It couldn't have just walked off!"

"I know what happened to it!" said Bill.

"What?" asked Gran.

"The same thing that happened to the kitten scraps and to Jelly Bean," said Bill.

"Oh, no!" said Liza. "Do you really think someone took Jelly Bean? We'll never see him again."

"Now just a minute," said Grandpa. "Jelly Bean might have followed whoever it was. But if someone has to rummage through garbage cans for food, he isn't going to take on a dog."

"Then that's worse," cried Liza. "He might hurt Jelly Bean or even kill him to get rid of him."

"Who says it's a he?" asked Bill.

"Stop it, Bill," said Liza. "Grandpa, we've got to do something! We've got to get Jelly Bean back."

"I know how you feel," said Grandpa, "but I don't know a thing we can do at the moment."

Liza left the table and ran upstairs to her room. Very quickly the boys also excused themselves.

7.

The Clue in the Berry Patch

"Gee," said Bill, "I wish we had some idea of what to do."

"Just a minute," said Jed. "I'm thinking about it."

Jed and Bill sat in silence for a few minutes.

"I think I know," said Jed.

"You do? Let me in on it!" said Bill.

"Well," said Jed, "if you were hiding around here, where would you hide?"

"Why the woods, of course," said Bill.

"Okay," said Jed. "So we need to go in the woods and see what we can find out."

"I don't know," said Bill. "I don't think Gran would go along with our going there. And I don't want to get into any more trouble with her."

"Yeah, I guess you're right," said Jed. "But there must be some way."

"Hey!" said Bill. "Those high bush blackberries! They should be ripe. I bet she'd go for some of those to make jelly."

"Good thinking!" said Jed. "We don't really have to go through the woods to get to that field, but we can just as well. Let's go tell Liza."

The boys raced upstairs to Liza's room. The door was closed, but they didn't wait to knock.

"Go away," said Liza.

"We've got a plan," said Bill.

Liza pretended not to listen. But the boys told her their plan anyway. All of a sudden she sat up.

"Maybe you're right!" she said. "Oh, maybe Jelly Bean is in the woods. Let's go. But do we have to pick blackberries?"

"Yep," said Jed. "That way maybe Gran won't say anything about our going so far from the house."

Liza washed her face and the three of them went downstairs.

"Say, Gran," said Bill, "shouldn't the high bush blackberries be ripe?"

"I was just thinking about them this morning," said Gran. "They should be ready. I would love to have some to make jelly."

"So we'll pick them for you," said Jed.

"Well," said Gran, "I don't know. With all these strange things happening around here, I don't really want you children going so far."

"We'll be careful," said Liza.

"What do you think, Grandpa?" asked Gran.

"If they promise to stay together, it will be all right," said Grandpa. "After all, there are three of them."

"Now did you hear your Grandpa?"

asked Gran. "You must stay together."

"We promise, Gran," said Bill.

"All right then," said Gran. "I would like to have the berries. But don't stay too late. Here, I'll get a pail for you."

Gran got the pail and gave it to Jed.

"Have fun!" called Grandpa.

"So it's off into the woods we go," said Bill.

"No," said Jed, "we're going to pick those berries. And it will be easier to do that first."

"Jed's right," said Liza. "It will take time to look for Jelly Bean. How could we ever explain being away so long if there were no berries?"

"Okay, okay," said Bill. "We'll just have to pick fast."

"And if you put them in the pail and not your mouth, we'll get through quicker," said Liza.

"Come on now! Have a heart," said Bill. "I've got to at least taste a few."

The children soon reached the field where the high bush berries grew. It had at one time been a pasture. Now it was not used, and berry bushes grew thickly at the edge of the woods.

"Hey, look at that," said Bill. "I've never seen so many berries at one time."

"Boy, it shouldn't take long to fill that pail," said Jed. "Let's get to work."

The children quickly began to pull the fruit and drop it into the pail.

Bill moved over to a new spot. He started to pick, and suddenly he stopped.

"Somebody else has been picking berries, too," he said.

"What? What?" said Jed. "I don't think anybody else even knows about this patch."

"Come and see for yourself," said Bill.

Jed and Liza moved over to where he was.

"See?" said Bill.

Sure enough, berries had been picked, and very recently. The stems were still fresh, showing where the berries had been.

"Maybe it was birds," said Liza. "They like berries."

"But birds don't pull the whole berry," said Jed. "They just pick at it like this."

Jed pointed to a berry that was half eaten.

"You don't think a bear is around, do you?" asked Bill.

"Bear!" cried Liza. "Let's go home."

"Don't be so dumb," said Jed. "There hasn't been a bear around here in years. Those berries were picked by somebody. And I think it's the somebody we are looking for. Come on, let's finish our picking."

The children picked just as fast as they could. Even Bill began to put all the berries into the pail. Soon the pail was better than half full.

"Okay," said Bill. "Surely Gran will be satisfied with these. I can't wait any longer."

"So let's go," said Jed. "But remember, we've got to stay right together in those woods."

"You don't have to worry about me!" said Liza. "I'm scared. Don't you think we should just go back the way we came?"

"Are you crazy or something?" asked

Bill. "You can go back the way you came. I'm going through those woods."

"Come on, Liza," said Jed, "be a sport. Don't you want to find Jelly Bean?"

Liza hesitated before she said, "Of course I do! But I would feel better if we had Grandpa with us."

"Girls!" said Bill. "She's going to spoil the whole thing."

"I'm not either," said Liza. "Come on, I'll go."

The boys breathed a sigh of relief.

"Try to be as quiet as you can," said Jed.

"That won't be hard," said Bill. "Those pine needles are like a carpet."

8.

Broken Twigs

The children started into the woods. Fire had destroyed many of the pines several years back. Other kinds of trees and thick tangly underbrush had replaced them.

It was so very quiet in the woods. Bits of sunlight filtered through the trees, making strange shadowy patterns on the ground below.

"It feels so creepy in here today," whispered Liza.

"Stick close to me," Jed whispered back.

The children walked slowly, looking carefully in every direction. But only a deep silence surrounded them.

Suddenly Jed stopped. He said, "Hold it a minute."

Jed began to retrace his path.

"What is it, Jed?" asked Bill.

Jed motioned for Bill and Liza to follow. They, too, retraced their path. Jed kept walking until he reached the edge of the woods again.

"What are you looking for, Jed?" Bill asked.

"Broken twigs," said Jed.

"Broken twigs!" said Liza, "What on earth for?"

"See this one?" said Jed. "All along the way I've been noticing bushes with one twig broken on them. I wanted to see where they started."

Bill walked a little ahead.

"Hey," he said, "there's another one over here."

The children looked more carefully as they walked. Every few yards they found a broken twig.

"Looks as if someone was marking a trail," said Liza.

"Yeah," said Bill. "Isn't that the way the Indians marked trails? Maybe there are still some around."

"For gosh sakes, Bill!" said Jed. "First you had bears, and now Indians. Before you know it you'll have a dinosaur or two around!"

"Now I would like that!" said Bill.

"Oh, come on, Bill," said Liza. "Be serious."

"Okay," said Bill, "so we've got a trail. Let's follow it."

"That's just what we're going to do," said Jed. "But keep your eyes open for other things as well."

When they were about half way through the woods, Bill stopped.

"Hey, look over there," he said. "There's something red."

Liza and Jed saw it. They stared at it.

"Bet that's your red sweater, Liza," said Jed.

"My red sweater!" said Liza. She felt her heart thumping. She was shaky all over.

"Come on," whispered Jed. He began to move along more quickly in the direction of the red. Bill followed right behind. Liza almost had to run to keep up. The patch of red did not move.

Suddenly Liza screamed. The boys looked back. Liza was sprawled on the ground.

"What happened?" asked Jed, running back.

"I—I tripped," said Liza.

"Well for gosh sakes get up," said Bill. "I knew you would spoil everything."

"But I couldn't help it," said Liza. "And I can't get up."

"Wait a minute," said Jed. "Your foot is caught under a root."

Jed pulled Liza back a bit. He slipped her foot out. Liza got up.

"You okay?" asked Jed.

"I think so," said Liza.

"No use to be quiet now. If anybody was around, he sure wouldn't be after all that screaming," said Bill. He began kicking at every stick he saw. Then he added, "And this time you can't blame me."

"I'm sorry," said Liza.

"Ah, cool down, Bill," said Jed. "Liza couldn't help it."

"At least that red thing is still there,"

said Bill. "Come on and let's see what it is before something else happens."

"Can you make it, Liza?" asked Jed.

"Yes," said Liza, "I'm coming."

Bill reached the place first. He called, "It's a sweater all right. It's caught on a bush, but I don't think it's Liza's. This one is a mess."

"I can soon tell," called Liza. But when she saw the sweater she stopped.

"Gosh, it sure is icky," she said. "It's so dirty and look at that big hole."

"It's not yours, is it?" asked Bill.

Liza took the sweater and looked inside it.

"Yes," she said, "it's mine."

And there indeed was a name tag that said, "Liza Roberts."

9.
A Cry in the Woods

"What are we going to do with this sweater now that we've found it?" asked Bill. "Gran would have a fit if we take it home."

"Put it back just where it was," said Jed. "Then we'll know if whoever took it comes back."

Jed hung the sweater on the low bush from which they had taken it.

"It can stay there forever for all I care," said Liza. "It's no good to me anymore."

"Gee," said Bill, "do you suppose whoever it is, is small enough to wear Liza's sweater?"

"Maybe there's more than one," said Jed. "Maybe one is a child."

"I hadn't thought of that," said Bill.

"Well, whoever it is sure doesn't take care of a sweater," said Liza.

"But we don't know what happened," said Jed. "The child may have had it on and been picking blackberries. Maybe the sweater got torn on the briars."

"Or maybe the child fell in the mud," said Bill. "Who knows?"

"Oh, well, there's nothing we can do about it now," said Liza. "Let's start following that trail again and see where it leads us."

The children started back along the trail. They had not gone far when they heard a whimpering sound. All three stopped. "What was that?" asked Jed.

"It sounded like somebody crying," said Liza. She grabbed Jed's arm. Bill moved in closer to the other two. The whimpering started again.

"I'm scared!" said Liza. "What should we do?"

"We've got to see what it is," said Jed. "Somebody may be hurt."

Bill took things in hand. He shouted, "Where are you?"

The whimpering changed to quick excited barks.

"Jelly Bean!" shouted the children and rushed in the direction of the barks. But they saw no signs of the black puppy.

"Where can he be?" said Liza. "Here Jelly Bean, here Jelly Bean."

Another series of barks answered her.

"Over here," called Jed. "I know they came from over here. Maybe he's caught in the bushes."

But as Jed neared the bushes, he heard the barks behind him. He turned and said, "Gee, he must be in a hole or something."

"Hey," said Bill, "I found him. He is in a hole, and it's almost covered with branches. That's why we couldn't see him."

Bill was throwing branches in all directions when Jed and Liza reached him. Jelly Bean was crying and barking and jumping all at the same time. Jed leaned over to get him.

"Can you reach him?" asked Liza.

"I could if he would just cooperate a

little and stop wiggling," said Jed. "Get on the other side and help me, Bill."

Both boys were lying on their stomachs trying to catch the wiggling excited puppy. Finally Jed succeeded.

"Oh, Jelly Bean!" cried Liza taking the puppy from Jed.

"Why are you crying now?" asked Bill.

"Because I'm so happy," said Liza.

"Oh, phooey!" said Bill, but there was a big smile on his face.

"Let's go home," said Liza.

"Wait a minute," said Jed. He was studying the hole from which they had rescued Jelly Bean.

Bill joined him. He said, "Gee, that is a strange hole."

"Hum," said Jed. "It's more than a hole. It's a trap. See how the sides go out as they go down? If an animal falls in, there is no way he can climb out. And remember the top of this one was covered with branches."

"But isn't that one of the ways the Indians used to trap animals?" asked Bill.

"Sure," said Jed. "But other people use it too."

"You mean that was a real trap Jelly Bean was in?" said Liza, "But who would do a thing like that?"

"Somebody who was hungry," said Jed. "I don't think they meant to trap Jelly Bean, but they sure meant to trap something."

"Oh, let's go home and tell Grandpa," said Liza. "This is getting to be too much mystery for me."

"Ah, girls!" said Bill.

"Maybe we should tell Gran and Grandpa," said Jed. "But let's wait a little longer. We'll come back tomorrow and see if we can't get to the bottom of this."

"But no more picking blackberries!" said Bill.

Jed laughed and said, "I agree! And I don't think we should mention the woods. Then nobody will think to tell us to stay out of them."

"But how can we explain about finding Jelly Bean?" asked Liza.

"Easily," said Bill. "Just say he fell in a hole. There are other holes around."

"All right," said Liza. "I don't care what you say. I'm so happy to have Jelly Bean back."

The children continued to follow the trail. Jelly Bean quieted down and seemed quite content to snuggle in Liza's arms.

"I bet this trail leads us right home," said Bill.

"No takers on that bet," said Jed. "There's the field back of the house right ahead."

In another few minutes the children were walking out of the woods. Something right at the edge caught Liza's eye.

"Hey, fellows, look," she called pointing to a low bush.

"Feathers!" said Bill. "Now why would anyone tie feathers to the top of a bush?"

Jed looked at the three blue feathers. Then he said, "I'll bet that's to show where the entrance to the trail is."

"Yeah," said Bill. "Then if whoever it is has to make a quick getaway he doesn't have to waste time looking for the trail."

"That scares me, that about a quick getaway," said Liza. "Let's hurry. I want to get home."

"Hey, Liza," called Jed. "Wait a minute! Now promise you won't tell."

Liza hesitated.

"At least promise you won't tell today," said Bill.

"Oh, all right," said Liza.

The three children hurried toward the house. Liza began shouting, "Gran! Grandpa! Come out and see what we found."

Gran and Grandpa came out on the porch.

"My goodness!" said Grandpa with a big smile. "Now that is a happy sight. Where did you find him?"

"He had fallen into a hole," said Bill. "Jed got him out."

Liza put Jelly Bean down, and he wiggled right over to Gran. Gran had to laugh at the funny puppy.

"He certainly doesn't seem to be any worse for the experience," she said.

"And look at these!" said Jed, putting

the pail of blackberries in front of Gran.

"Look, Grandpa! What a fine lot of berries," said Gran. "Now if you boys will go right out to the barn and find me about a dozen jelly glasses, I'll get started on these right away. Oh, and Liza, I think that little pup would be happy to see a dish of food."

"Children," called Grandpa, "before you do anything, take a look in the dining room."

The three went into the dining room.

"The lamp!" said Bill. "It's all fixed."

"Yes," said Grandpa. "Better than it was before."

"Gran, I'm so glad," said Liza and gave Gran a big hug.

Gran kissed Liza on the cheek and said, "Now you children go on about your business. I want to wash those berries so they can be cooking while I get supper ready."

Liza fed the puppy while the boys went in search of the glasses. Gran was right.

Jelly Bean was happy to see food. For once he was so busy eating that he forgot to wiggle.

"Here are the glasses," said Bill.

"Thank you, boys," said Gran. "Just put them in that dish pan."

"I'll wash them," said Liza.

"Fine," said Gran. "That will be a help."

"What can we do to help?" asked Jed.

"Well, you can help me clean these berries," said Gran.

Liza filled the dishpan with warm soapy water. She began to play around with the suds and forgot about washing the glasses.

A little later Gran said, "There, that's done. Now I'll just add a little water and let them cook."

Gran brought a pitcher over to the sink.

"My goodness, Liza," she said, "what on earth are you doing? Where are the jelly glasses?"

Liza jumped.

"Oh, Gran," she said, "you scared me. I guess I was daydreaming. I was having so much fun with the soap suds, I forgot about the glasses."

Gran laughed and said, "Well, just move over long enough for me to get a pitcher of water."

After that Liza quickly washed the glasses. Then she began to set the table for supper.

"What are we having tonight?" asked Bill.

"Stew," said Gran. "The kind you like."

"Ummmm," said Bill, "let's eat."

"If you like half-cooked stew, all right," said Gran. "Otherwise you three just run along and let me get organized."

"We get the message," said Jed. "Come on, let's go."

Before the children could leave, they heard Grandpa say, "Now I declare!"

10.

Disappearing Children

All attention turned to Grandpa.

"What is it?" asked Gran.

"Two children over in Brookdale disappeared," said Grandpa.

"Disappeared!" said Gran. "When?"

"A couple of days ago," said Grandpa.

Liza, Jed, and Bill crowded around Grandpa to look over his shoulder.

"Is that them?" asked Bill.

"Yes," said Grandpa, "and such young tykes, too!"

On the front page of the paper was a large picture of two children. The boy looked to be about Jed's age, and the girl was younger than Liza.

"What does it say?" asked Bill.

"It says," began Grandpa, " 'Two Brookdale children, Paul and Melissa Martin, disappear after a quarrel with their stepmother. The father, who travels much of the time, is in Europe on business. The stepmother says the children are often difficult when he is away. When they were angry, the children ran away and went to the home of their father's two elderly aunts. The aunts had taken care of the children after their mother's death until their father's remarriage.

" 'Lunchtime came, and the children did not return. But when they hadn't returned by dark, the stepmother began to worry. She tried to call the aunts, but got no answer. Both of the old ladies are quite deaf. They never hear the telephone unless they are in the same room with it. The stepmother went over to their house. But the aunts had not seen the children all day. She called all the neighbors. No one had seen the children. She called the police. They checked the bus and train stations. No one had seen the children. Searching parties are scouring the woods in the area. But thus far, no sign of the children.' "

"Gee," said Jed. "Grandpa, how far away is Brookdale?"

"About seventy or so miles," said Grandpa.

"Those poor children," said Gran. "I do hope they are found soon."

"I don't!" said Liza. "I bet their stepmother was mean to them."

"She must have been mean," said Bill. "Remember, the children had run away before."

"But she said they were difficult children," said Grandpa.

"Difficult phooey!" said Bill. "I'm with Liza. I hope she never finds them."

"But, children," said Gran, "they are too young to look out for themselves. Let's hope they are found before anything happens to them."

"No," said Liza. "If they find them, they'll send them back to that dreadful stepmother."

Suddenly Bill jumped up.

"I'll bet you anything . . ." he started, but stony stares from Jed and Liza stopped him.

"I'll bet you anything, too," said Jed, "that we forgot to close the barn door when we got those jelly glasses. Come on."

"But that's not what I was going to say," said Bill.

Jed was right by him then. He whispered, "Cut it out, Bill, before you ruin everything."

The children quickly left the room and went outside.

"Why did you stop me?" said Bill angrily. "You always act as if you know everything."

"You were about to say you bet it was those children taking the kitten scraps, weren't you?" asked Jed.

"So what if I was?" said Bill. "Why shouldn't I have said that?"

"*Why?*" said Liza. "Do you want those children to go back to that horrible person?"

"What does one have to do with the other?" asked Bill.

"Don't be so stupid!" said Jed. "If you told Gran and Grandpa, what would be the first thing they would do?"

Bill was silent.

"You see," said Liza, "they would feel they had to tell the police. Then look what would happen."

Bill kicked a stone and said, "But what are we going to do?"

"I don't know," said Jed, "but we'll think of something."

11.

No More Scraps

A little later Gran called everybody to the table. There was not much conversation that night. Gran's stew was a favorite meal. Besides being too busy eating to talk, the children had so much to think about.

After supper Gran said, "You children have had quite a day. I'll clean up the kitchen. I have to strain the berry juice anyway."

"Oh, no, Gran," said Liza. "We'll help. We can wash the other dishes and get them out of your way."

"If you really feel like it," said Gran, "that will be fine."

Gran went to the stove and cut off the heat under the berries.

"I'll just let these cool while you do the dishes," she said. "Now don't forget to save the scraps for the kittens."

"And for the mysterious thief," said Bill.

"No!" said Gran firmly. "I'm sick and tired of this nonsense. No more scraps in the garbage can! If there's nothing there, then these pranks will stop."

"But, Gran," protested Bill.

"No," said Gran, "and that's definite."

"But, Gran," started Bill again. Liza poked him.

"All right, Gran," she said. "No more scraps in the garbage can."

Jed understood what Liza was saying and quickly said, "That's right, Gran. We promise. No more scraps in the garbage can."

"Thank you," said Gran. "I knew you

children would be sensible about it."

Gran left the kitchen.

Bill was still spluttering. "Okay, now what's all that about?" he asked crossly.

"Bill, didn't you hear what Gran said?" asked Liza.

"Oh, come off it," said Bill. "You know I heard what she said as well as you did. She said, 'No more scraps in the garbage can.'"

"All right," said Jed. "So we'll not leave any more scraps. Do you call that good food we left last night 'scraps'?"

Bill grinned and said, "I guess I'm just not quick enough. I see what you mean. But what if Gran finds out?"

"She won't," said Jed. "This is the last time we'll do it. Tomorrow we'll figure out another way to get food to those children. Maybe we'll even find them!"

"I know," said Liza. "Let's leave them a note tonight."

"Now that's a good idea," said Bill. "I'll write it."

"Okay," said Liza, "but we've got to hurry. Gran may be back any minute."

"You're right," said Jed. "Liza, you find some food, and I'll put the kitten scraps into a bag while Bill writes the note."

Liza went to the refrigerator and quickly pulled out all sorts of food. She just as quickly put them into a plastic bag and tied the top.

"Okay," she said. "All ready."

"And the note is ready, too," said Bill.

"Here, let me see what you wrote," said Liza.

Bill handed her the note. Liza read, "We know who you are and we want to help you. Your friends, Liza, Bill, and Jed Roberts."

"That should do it," said Jed. "I'll take it out."

"But hurry!" said Liza.

"And be quiet," said Bill.

Jed did both, and in no time at all the children were busily washing the dishes. Gran came in just as they were finishing.

"My, what a neat job," she said. "Don't worry about the berry things. I can clean them up, and I think your Grandpa would like to have some company on the porch."

The children started out of the kitchen, but Gran called, "Liza, perhaps the puppy should sleep in here for a night or so. We don't want to go through another day like this one."

"Gran!" said Liza, "do you really mean it? Oh, Gran, I'm so happy."

Liza went out on the back porch. She brought the puppy and box inside. Jelly Bean woke up just enough to stick out a pink tongue. Then his eyes closed again. Liza put the box in a corner of the kitchen.

"There now," said Gran, "I think we'll all feel better about that pup. He is very little."

Liza didn't say anything. She hugged Gran quickly. Then she went out on the front porch to join Grandpa and the boys.

But Grandpa was not on the porch. Liza saw a truck parked down the lane. It was too dark to see who it was.

"Who's Grandpa talking to?" she asked.

"Mr. Sanders," said Jed. "They're talking about some business."

The children sat quietly for a few minutes. Suddenly Liza clapped her hand over her mouth.

"Oh!" she said.

"Oh, what?" asked Bill.

"Gran is straining the blackberries!" said Liza.

"So?" said Bill.

"But when she does that she has all that gooky pulp left over," said Liza. "And suppose she decides to put it in the garbage can!"

"Gosh, we would be goners for sure," said Jed jumping up. "We'd better get in the kitchen."

The children had a hard time not running. But they knew Gran would suspect something if they did.

"Deserting your Grandpa?" asked Gran.

"He deserted us," said Jed. "He and Mr. Sanders are talking."

"Oh," said Gran. "Well, I'll be through just as soon as I put this pulp in the garbage can."

82

Gran picked up the newspaper-wrapped pulp.

"Here, Gran," said Jed. "We can do that. Come on, Bill, help me."

The two boys took out the pulp. Gran washed her hands.

"Now, that's all done," she said. "And tomorrow it won't take long to make the juice into jelly."

Liza yawned. The busy day and last night's late hours were catching up with her.

"I think I'll go to bed," she said as the boys came in the door.

"I'm going to do the same thing as soon as Grandpa comes in," said Gran.

Liza went over to take one last look at Jelly Bean. He was sleeping just as contentedly as a baby. She started toward the stairs.

"We're going to bed, too," said Jed. "Wait for us, Liza."

The children started upstairs.

"Whew!" said Jed. "We just got to the kitchen in time."

"Yep," said Bill. "You know, Liza, sometimes you make a pretty good twin sister."

"Gee, thanks," said Liza, and ducked into her room before Bill could pull her hair.

It was not long before all the lights were out. The children were too tired to even wonder if their note would be answered. Liza's last thoughts were of Jelly Bean. At least she could be sure the wiggly black puppy would be there to greet her the next morning.

12.

Show-Off Puppy

Liza was the first of the three children to reach the kitchen the next morning. What she saw made her stop in her tracks. There was Gran shaking her head and laughing at the same time. The kitchen floor was covered with dish towels.

"Gran!" said Liza. "What on earth happened?"

Gran was chuckling so hard she could hardly answer.

"Wait a second," she said. "You'll see."

Suddenly a high-stepping Jelly Bean popped out from under the stove. He was shaking a towel as hard as he could. Grandpa, Jed, and Bill had reached the kitchen by then. Everybody roared with laughter. Jelly Bean seemed to know he was in the spotlight. He put on quite a show.

"Gran," said Liza, "how did he ever manage this?"

"Somebody left the towel drawer open a bit," said Gran, "and this nosey puppy figured out the rest on his own. Thank goodness I remembered to close the kitchen door. Can you image what this house would be like?"

"I'll help you wash the towels," said Liza.

"Oh, nonsense," said Gran. "I'll just pitch them in the washing machine. There's no harm done. But we'll have to be more careful about not leaving anything open."

Gran was still chuckling. Jed, Bill, and Liza looked at each other. Gran was really full of surprises. She had not even wanted the puppy to set foot inside. Now she was laughing at this mess.

Suddenly Bill went over to Gran and hugged her. He said, "Gran, you're just a big fake. All that talk about a dog not belonging inside."

Gran's eyes twinkled as she said, "Well, most dogs don't. But this one is terribly small. I guess he needs special care."

"Gran," said Jed, "you're just a softy."

"Now you children just stop that," said Gran. "You're not supposed to find out all my secrets."

The children laughed and began to pick up the towels.

"Wait a minute," said Gran. "Liza, that one looks terribly worn. Let me have it."

Liza handed Gran the towel. Gran quickly tied some large knots in it.

"After all," she said, "little pups need something to play with. Here, put him outside with this."

Jed caught the wiggling puppy. All three children went outside. Jed put the puppy down with his towel. Jelly Bean quite happily began to shake it around.

"Hey!" said Jed. "Let's see if they took the food and our note."

The children ran toward the garbage can. All three stopped short as they reached it.

"Well, look at that, would you!" said Bill.

There, sitting on top of the garbage can, was a clump of wild flowers. And on the ground, spelled out in sticks, was the word, *thanks*.

"Oh, those darling children!" said Liza. "Let's get Gran and Grandpa."

"Get Gran and Grandpa!" said Jed. "That really would blow the whole thing."

"Gee, I forgot that time," said Liza. "But do let's plant the flowers. I can't bear for them just to die."

"Okay, but hurry it up," said Jed. "We've got to make plans."

"Where should I plant them?" asked Liza.

"Why not right here?" said Bill. "Just dig a hole and stick them in."

"Come on, Bill!" said Jed. "Gran would be sure to see them there, and they wouldn't live anyway. They're woods plants, and they need shade."

"I know just the place," said Liza. "Get the trowel and some water."

But just then Gran called, "Breakfast, children."

"Okay," said Jed. "Right after breakfast."

As soon as the children had eaten, they gathered up the things they needed and Liza led the way.

"Here," she said, "under the lilac bush. It's always shady and damp here."

Jed dug a hole, and Liza set the clump of flowers in it.

"Now pour the water around them, Bill," she said.

"Okay, here goes," said Bill. He dumped the whole pot of water right on top of the plants.

"Bill, stop it," said Liza. "You'll drown them."

"Huh!" said Bill. "Now I've heard everything. A plant drowning!"

"That's enough of that," said Jed. "We've got to figure out some way to get food to those children."

"I know," said Liza. "Let's leave some where we found the red sweater."

"That's a good idea," said Bill.

"But how can we get food without Gran knowing? She's in the kitchen now making that blackberry jelly," said Jed.

"Don't worry," said Liza. "I'll take care of that. You and Bill wait here."

"Do you think maybe we should leave another note?" asked Bill.

"I hadn't thought of that," said Jed. "Why don't we write the note while Liza gets the food?"

"Let's go," said Bill. "I'm a good note writer."

The children went into the kitchen. Jed and Bill went on upstairs.

"Gran," said Liza, "may I fix some sandwiches?"

"Sandwiches!" said Gran. "You children just had breakfast. Where do you put all this food?"

"We thought we would take a long hike," said Liza, "and you know how hungry that makes you."

"It might be a good idea after all," said Gran. "I found I didn't have enough sugar to do the jelly. Grandpa has gone into town for some. Lunch will probably be a little late. Go ahead and make your sandwiches."

Liza made several peanut butter and jelly sandwiches. She saw some boiled eggs and took two of them. For good measure she added a handful of cookies and put the lunch in a bag.

About that time the boys came downstairs.

"Okay," said Liza. "The lunch is ready."

"Lunch?" asked Bill.

"For the hike!" said Liza. "You're always the one to get hungry."

"What . . ." Bill started to say, but Jed pulled him toward the door.

"We'll be back later, Gran," he said.

When they got outside, Jed turned to Bill and said, "Sometimes you act so dumb."

"But nobody told me about any lunch or hike," said Bill.

"What did you think I was going to tell Gran?" asked Liza. "That we wanted some food to leave in the woods?"

"You know I've got better sense than that!" said Bill.

"Sometimes I wonder," said Liza.

"Oh, well," said Jed, "Gran didn't seem to notice. Let's go."

13.

The Long Watch

The children started through the woods toward the spot where they had found the red sweater.

"The sweater's gone," said Liza.

"Good," said Jed. "That means Paul and Melissa are still around"

"I wish we could remember just which bush we found the sweater on," said Liza. "It would be fun to leave the food in exactly the same spot."

Jed got on his hands and knees. He looked around for a bit. Then he said, "This is it."

"How do you know?" asked Liza. "One bush looks just like another to me."

"Come and see," said Jed.

Bill and Liza went over to the bush.

"See those three stones?" said Jed. "I remember seeing them before."

"But why didn't you say something about it?" said Liza. "Maybe that was a clue."

"Yeah, clue all right," said Bill. "You put those stones there, Jed Roberts. I saw you do it just a minute ago."

Liza looked startled.

"Jed!" she said. "You didn't do that, did you?"

Bill looked at Jed suspiciously.

"I'll bet this whole thing is your doing," he said. "You've probably been taking the kitten scraps. And you were the one who thought of those broken twigs to mark that trail. Is this your idea of a good joke?"

This time it was Jed who looked startled.

"Me!" he said "You know I wouldn't do that!"

"Oh, wouldn't you?" said Bill. "You just lied about those stones."

"All right, all right," said Jed. "I'll admit that. But I had nothing to do with taking the kitten scraps or the trail or anything else."

Bill still didn't look convinced.

"That was a dirty trick!" he said. "Are you sure you're telling the truth now?"

"Cross my heart and hope to die!" said Jed.

"Well," Bill muttered, "I guess this bush is as good as any. Give me the food and I'll tie it on."

Liza handed him the bag and he fastened it to the bush.

"Where's the note?" asked Jed.

"In my pocket," said Bill, and pulled out a folded piece of paper.

"What does the note say?" asked Liza.

Bill handed the piece of paper to Liza. She unfolded it and read, "Please come out so we can talk to you. We will bring more food to the same place later. Jed, Bill, and Liza."

"Okay?" asked Bill.

"Yes," said Liza. "Do you think they really will come out and talk to us?"

"Who knows?" said Jed. "But we should get out of the way and let them find it. Let's go."

Jed started back the way they had come.

Bill caught up with him. "You crazy or something?" he said. "We're not going back to the house, are we?"

"Shh, you idiot," said Jed. "Just follow me."

Bill and Liza followed Jed. He acted as if he was leading them back to the house. Then suddenly he cut off back of a clump of bushes.

Jed whispered, "Okay, we can watch from here. I don't think anybody can see us. But remember, quiet is the word."

Quickly and quietly the three children settled down. Their eyes were glued to that bag of food hanging from the bush.

The children sat for a very long time. Nothing happened. The silence was broken only by the rustling of leaves and the twittering of birds.

Liza whispered, "My legs are getting crampy."

"Try to shift around and stretch them out," Jed whispered back.

A little later Bill jumped up.

"I've had enough," he shouted. "If those children don't want those sandwiches, I do. I'm starved."

He started out of the thicket. Jed grabbed his arm.

"Well, that fixes that," Jed said angrily.

"I don't care," said Bill. "I'm going to get something to eat."

"You're not going to eat those sandwiches," said Liza. "You're just not going to do it."

"We might as well go home," said Jed. "You talk about other people spoiling things!"

The children started toward home. Each one was caught up in his own thoughts.

"You know," said Liza finally, "I had the creepiest feeling that all the time those children were watching us."

"That's funny," said Jed. "I had that same feeling. Maybe that's why they didn't take the food."

"You're just imagining things," said Bill. "If they knew we were just more children, why wouldn't they come out? They should have known we wouldn't hurt them."

"Yes," said Jed, "but we could tell on them. I'll bet they are scared."

"Oh," said Liza, "I wish we could do something for them."

"We're doing all we can," said Bill. "Now Liza, don't you start crying."

"I can't help it," said Liza.

Jed stopped. He said, "You'll have to help it. If we tell now, we'll never be able to help those children."

"Yeah," said Bill, "and you know Gran! If you cry, she's going to find out why."

"All right," said Liza. "But can we go back this afternoon and see if they found the note?"

"Go back!" shouted Bill. "Of course we're going back!"

"Maybe after they read the note they will believe us and come out," said Jed.

"Okay," said Liza. "I'll race you to the house."

The boys grinned. They knew Liza could keep the secret now. They all ran toward the house.

14.

Jelly Bean Gets a Bath

The three children hit the back steps at about the same time. Bill shouted, "Hey, Gran, we're home."

"There's no doubt about that," Gran called back. "Come in and see the jelly."

The children went into the kitchen. On the shelf stood eleven glasses of shimmering blackberry jelly.

"Ummm," said Bill. "That does look good."

"Grandpa!" said Liza. "What are you doing?"

"Being the chef," said Grandpa. "Gran was busy with the jelly. I thought I'd just make some sandwiches for lunch."

"I hope you children don't mind more sandwiches," said Gran.

"More sandwiches!" said Bill. Liza quickly poked him and he remembered. He said, "We never get tired of sandwiches."

"Oh, Jelly Bean!" said Gran. "Do get from under my feet."

The children looked down in surprise.

"Jelly Bean in the house?" said Liza.

"Sure," said Jed. "Every time Gran said 'jelly' he probably thought she meant him."

"Or either that it was something *for* him," said Bill. "You know – jelly for Jelly Bean."

Gran and Grandpa were both laughing.

"Well, I don't know what he thought," said Gran, "but he does love company. He's been under my feet all morning."

The three children grinned at each other. They could tell by Gran's voice, she hadn't really minded Jelly Bean being under her feet.

"All right," said Grandpa. "Sandwiches are ready."

Everybody sat down and dived into the sandwiches.

"My goodness," said Gran, "one would think you children hadn't eaten in hours. I don't know why you aren't as fat as pigs."

Grandpa chuckled and said, "The way they stay on the go there's no chance of that."

"Here," said Gran. "Do try some of the jelly."

"The new jelly!" said Bill. "Oh boy, pass me the bread."

Bill spread butter on the bread and added a thick layer of jelly.

"Now that's real eating," he said. "I guess it was worth picking those berries after all."

Soon everybody had finished eating.

"After the dishes are done," said Gran, "I want you children to give this puppy a bath."

"A bath!" said the children in surprise. "Why?"

"Because he has fleas," said Gran. "And I won't have a puppy in this house with fleas."

"But isn't he too little for a bath?" asked Liza.

"No," said Gran. "I called Mr. Sanders. He brought over some soap to wash him with and some powder to put on him. He said it would be all right to bathe him if I kept him inside."

There weren't many dishes, so the kitchen was soon ready for Jelly Bean's bath. Gran put a small tub in the sink and said, "This should be about the right size. Now don't get the water too hot."

Liza ran some water in the tub.

"Gran, feel this," she said. "I don't think it's too hot."

"No," said Gran, "that feels about right."

"Okay," said Liza. "Somebody catch Jelly Bean."

Jelly Bean seemed to know that something was about to happen. He played a merry game of chase with Bill and Jed. Finally they caught him.

"He's so wiggly," said Liza. "One of you hold him and I'll try to put the soap on."

Jelly Bean didn't like this one bit. He wiggled and he squirmed and he splashed. But finally the children were able to wash and rinse him.

"Here," said Gran, holding out a soft towel. "Put him in this."

Gran rubbed him thoroughly with the towel and put him on the floor. Jelly Bean began to run. Then he stopped and shook himself and ran some more. He had everybody laughing.

"He may not have liked that bath. But he sure feels good now," said Bill.

"We'll let him dry now," said Gran, "and then I want you children to rub in that powder. I've already sprinkled his bed with it."

"All right, Gran," said Jed.

"In the meantime," said Gran, "Sarah called and said she was coming over to

help me this afternoon instead of tomorrow. So I want you children to go up and take the sheets off your beds. I can start washing them, and Sarah can put on the fresh ones. And take a good look around your rooms to make sure there are no stray socks or such."

"Yes, Gran," said Liza.

The children started upstairs.

"Gee," said Bill. "Gran is sure full of ideas."

"Oh, well," said Jed, "none of this will take very long."

"And as soon as Sarah comes, Gran will want us out of the way," said Liza.

15.

The Unsuccessful Hunt

Finally the chores were all done. Jelly Bean had been rubbed with flea powder. He was snoozing in his box. The children were free to go about their own business.

"See you later, Gran," called Bill.

"All right," said Gran. "But don't go too far. It seems to be clouding up."

The children walked toward the woods.

"Do you think the food will be gone?" asked Liza.

"Of course it will, silly," said Bill. "Why shouldn't it be?"

"Well," said Jed, "we'll soon know. Let's hurry."

The children stopped talking and

walked faster. Soon they came in sight of the place where they had left the food. But the bag was hanging just where they had left it.

"Oh, no!" said Liza. "They didn't find it after all."

"But where's the note?" asked Bill. "I stuck it in the top of the bag, and I don't see it."

"Gee, maybe they *did* find it," said Jed.

"But why would they take the note and not the food?" asked Liza.

"I don't know," said Jed. "Let's look around and see if we can find out."

The children went over to the bush, but they saw nothing to give them a clue why the children would take the note and not the food.

"Hey, wait a minute," said Bill. He went crawling under a bush. When he came out, he said, "Well, here's the note."

"Gosh, do you think they found it and

threw it away?" asked Liza. "Maybe they were afraid to take the food."

"For pete's sake why?" asked Bill.

"Maybe they thought it was some kind of a trap," said Liza.

Then Jed said, "Or maybe the note just fell off and the wind blew it under that bush. It wasn't tied on, you know."

Bill and Liza looked surprised. Liza said, "Yes, that could have happened."

"But gosh," said Bill, "how will we ever know if they're still here?"

"We'll just have to keep trying to find them," said Jed. "They were here this morning, so there's no reason to think they aren't still. They just may not have been where we left the food."

"Well, I'm getting tired of all this hiding. If they are here, I'm going to find them and right now," shouted Bill.

He picked up a big stick and began beating the bushes.

"Stop it!" shouted Liza. "You'll never get them to come out that way."

"No," said Jed. "You'll only scare them more."

"So what do you plan to do?" asked Bill.

"Let's search the woods the best we can," said Liza.

The children walked all through the woods. As they went they softly called, "Paul, Melissa, please let us help you."

But there was no answering call.

Later Bill said, "Gosh, I think we've

covered every step of these woods. Where could they be?"

"I don't know," said Jed. "I need to sit down and think this out."

He walked over to a big rock and sat. The other two joined him. For a while they sat in silence.

Finally Jed said, "You know, those children might not be in these woods after all."

"What do you mean?" asked Liza. "This is where we found my red sweater, and it's our kitten scraps they've been taking."

"Yeah," said Bill, "and this is where we found the trail."

"It's that trail I was thinking about," said Jed. "Do you remember where it started?"

"Sure," said Bill. "It started at the edge and went straight through the woods."

"What are you getting at, Jed?" asked Liza. "I don't understand."

"They could be in Mr. Baker's woods across the pasture just as well," said Jed, "couldn't they?"

Bill and Liza didn't say anything for a minute. Then Bill said, "Yes, I guess they could at that."

"But my sweater," said Liza. "That wasn't on the trail."

"I know," said Jed. "I still don't understand about that sweater."

"Let's go look anyway," said Bill. "It can't hurt anything."

The children started through the woods again. But suddenly it began to get dark.

"It couldn't be night already, could it?" asked Liza.

As if in answer to her question there was a flash of lightning followed by a loud roll of thunder.

"It's not night!" said Jed. "But it sure is going to rain. We'd better hurry."

16.
To Tell or Not to Tell

Even though the children ran, they were not able to beat the rain. By the time they reached the edge of the woods it was pouring. They dashed for the back porch. Gran heard them and came to the door.

"You poor things! You're soaked!" she said. "Take off your shoes and socks. I'll get some towels."

Gran handed them each a towel and the children dried themselves the best they could.

"Oh, I'm freezing," said Liza.

"And well you might be," said Gran. "Now run upstairs, take a hot bath, and get into some dry clothes."

By the time the children came back downstairs, Gran had supper on the table.

As they sat down to eat, Grandpa said, "Oh, by the way, Gran, I spoke to Mr. Sanders. He can take that old elm down next week if we want him to. But we have to let him know as soon as we can."

"I do hate to see that tree go," said Gran, "but it is getting dangerous."

Gran and Grandpa continued to discuss whether the tree should or should not come down. The children were just as glad they didn't have to join in the conversation. They had more important things to think about.

After supper everybody went into the front room. Jed and Bill started a game of checkers. Liza curled up in a chair by herself.

Outside the rain was still pouring.

"My, it is nice to be inside on a night like this," said Gran.

Liza looked very unhappy. Gran kept glancing over at her. Finally she said, "Liza, dear, I think something is bothering you. Don't you want to tell Gran about it?"

With that Liza began crying. Gran went over and put her arms around Liza.

"There now," said Gran. "Let's talk about it. I think I know what's wrong."

Bill and Jed looked at each other.

Gran went on, "I think you're just

homesick! But you know it won't be long before your parents will be here."

"Wow!" whispered Bill. "That was close. I really thought Gran knew."

"Shhh!" said Jed.

"But, Gran!" said Liza. "It's those children I'm worried about. They're out in all of this rain."

"Oh, oh," whispered Bill. "She's going to tell now for sure."

"Eh? What's that?" asked Grandpa. "What children?"

"Those two from Brookdale," said Liza. "The ones who disappeared."

"My goodness!" said Grandpa. "Didn't you know? They showed up again the same day that story was in the paper. You mean you've been worrying about them all this time?"

"But . . ." Liza started and then stopped herself.

"Then who . . ." started Bill. He was stopped by a look from Jed.

"Who found them?" asked Jed.

"Nobody," said Grandpa. "They just came back by themselves. They had been hiding out at their great-aunts' all the time."

"But how could they manage?" asked Liza.

"They knew the habits of the old ladies very well," said Grandpa. "And since both of them were quite deaf, the children managed to slip around without their knowing it. They stayed in the basement or the attic a lot of the time. The aunts never went to either of these places. Then when the aunts were outside or resting, the two got food. But they got bored with the whole thing and went home."

"Oh, for gosh sakes!" said Bill. He picked up the checker board and dumped the checkers into the box. Then he said, "Phooey, I'm bored with checkers. Let's go upstairs."

Without a word, Jed and Liza followed.

The children were indeed troubled as they gathered in Liza's room.

"If it's not those children," said Bill, "who is it?"

Liza turned to Jed and said, "Jed, are you sure it wasn't you?"

"Oh, for gosh sakes!" said Jed. "Are you still thinking about that one little trick! For the last time, no! I had nothing to do with anything else."

"Then it must be Indians after all," said Bill. But after seeing the look on Jed's and Liza's faces, he quickly added, "Or a fugitive."

"Do you think a fugitive would bring us flowers and leave us a message?"

"He might," said Bill. "Whoever it is must have some reason for hiding."

"That red sweater is what puzzles me," said Jed. "I still think there must be a child."

"Well, I'm scared!" said Liza. "I'm going down and tell Gran and Grandpa."

"Wait a minute, Liza," said Bill. "Let's talk this thing over some more. What do you think we should do, Jed?"

"I don't know," said Jed. "I want to tell. Still, I think we should wait for one more day."

"Wait for what?" asked Liza.

"I'm not sure," said Jed. "I just have a funny feeling that we should."

"I'm with Jed," said Bill. "Grandpa couldn't do anything tonight anyway. He and Gran would just worry."

Liza was silent.

"Wait one more day," said Jed. "If we don't figure it out tomorrow, we'll tell. Agreed?"

"Agreed!" said Bill.

Liza still looked doubtful. Then she said, "Well, okay — because I don't think anybody really bad would have left those flowers."

17.

Frightened Children

The next morning Gran had a few chores for the children to do, but it wasn't long before they were free to go their own way.

As they walked, Bill said, "Okay, now what's our plan?"

"Let's try to sneak through the woods, not along that trail, but close enough to it so we can see if anyone comes," said Jed. "There are enough bushes that we should be able to do it without being seen."

"But how will we ever get across the pasture?" asked Liza.

"I don't know," said Jed. "We'll worry about that when we get there. First things first, you know, and these woods are first. Try to go as quietly as you can, and don't talk unless you really need to."

The children moved quickly and quietly, ducking from one bush to the next. Their eyes were always on the trail, but no one came along. Finally they were through the woods.

"Now what?" asked Bill.

The children stood behind the berry bushes and looked across the open pasture. They knew that on the other side the land sloped quite sharply as it led into the woods on Mr. Baker's place. Grandpa said that a river had probably once run through there and that was why the land was so much lower. From Grandpa's woods the children could see only the tops of the trees.

"Oh, we'll never get to the other side without being seen," said Liza.

"I think we can," said Jed. "These

weeds are pretty high and there are lots of bushes along the way. If we keep low we can make it."

"Besides that," said Bill, "if they're in the woods they can't see us anyway."

"Okay," said Jed. "Keep low—and go!"

Little by little the children made their way across the pasture.

"Gee," said Bill, "this is exciting."

"Scary is my word for it," said Liza.

"Well, we'll soon be there," said Jed. "See that thicket right at the edge? I think we'd better head for it. That will give us good cover, and we should be able to see into the woods as well."

The children had to cross a fairly wide stretch with no bushes in order to reach the thicket. They had to concentrate on staying low enough not to be seen. But at last they reached their goal.

Liza peered through the bushes. Then she rubbed her eyes and whispered, "It can't be! It can't be real!"

But one look at Bill's and Jed's faces told her they were seeing the same thing, and it was real.

"Jeepers!" said Bill. "An Indian camp!"

And there below them in a clearing at the edge of the woods was an Indian tepee. In front of the tepee a fire burned, and over the fire hung a pot in which something was cooking. To one side was a large Indian drum.

The children stared in disbelief. And as they stared a boy and a girl ran out of the tepee. They were closely followed by a man and a woman.

"My gosh! Real Indians!" said Jed. "And look at the way they're all painted up."

"Yeah," said Bill. "Just as if they're on the warpath!"

"Oh, they look so—so savage!" said Liza.

"I think we'd better go," said Jed.

But no one moved. No one could take

his eyes from the scene that was taking place before them.

The man walked over to the drum and began a slow rhythmic beat. The woman picked up some rattles and joined in. Then the children began to dance around the drum. The man speeded up the beat. And as the children speeded up their

steps they began to let out wild, blood-curdling whoops.

Liza scooted in between Jed and Bill and held tightly to both of them.

Suddenly the dancing stopped. The boy ran over and picked up a bow. Then the children saw an arrow arch gracefully in the air and come to rest in the side of the hill.

The boy shot another arrow. This time it landed not too far from the thicket where the children were hiding. They could see the arrow shaft with its bright feathers sticking out of the hillside.

"Golly!" said Bill. "That's for real! He's shooting at us now!"

"I don't think so," said Jed. "At least he wasn't looking in our direction."

"Let's try to make it to that next thicket," said Bill.

"Okay, but crawl," said Jed.

Wordlessly Liza followed the boys as

they scuttled on all fours to the next thicket.

They had just got there when they heard a loud "Wahoo!" The boy and girl were running up the hill.

"Oh, oh!" said Liza. "They've seen us!"

"Better run!" said Bill.

"No," said Jed. "Keep still."

"Oh," said Liza with relief. "They're just looking for the arrows."

"Boy," said Bill, "am I glad we moved! Did you see how close to that other thicket he went? We would have been goners!"

"Okay," said Jed. "As soon as they go back, we're going to take off."

The three children watched the boy and girl gather the arrows and run down the hill toward their camp.

"Now!" said Jed, and the children started moving. As soon as they had gone a little way they forgot about being quiet. They tried to keep low, but what they each most wanted was to get across that pasture quickly and safely. Never had a short journey seemed so long!

When they finally reached the woods, Liza just flopped on the ground.

"Hey, none of that," said Jed. "We've still got to get through these woods."

"Let's run," said Bill.

And run they did until Liza called, "Please, please wait! I just can't run any farther."

"I think it's safe now," said Jed. They waited for Liza and walked until they were out of the woods.

Then, without a word, all three ran toward the house.

As they went in the door, Liza yelled, "Gran! Grandpa!"

"Not so loud," called Gran. "We're right here."

Liza flung her arms around Gran and burst into tears.

"Liza!" said Gran. "What on earth is

wrong? Why, you're shaking all over!"

"All three of you look as if you've seen a ghost," said Grandpa.

"I think we've seen several!" said Bill.

"Grandpa, there are Indians in Mr. Baker's woods!" said Jed.

"Indians!" exclaimed Grandpa.

"Yeah," said Bill. "And they shot arrows at us."

"Shot arrows at you!" said Grandpa.

"Now wait a minute, Bill," said Jed. "They weren't shooting at us. But they were shooting arrows."

"That one sure came close," said Bill.

"And their faces were all painted and they did a war dance," said Liza. "Oh, it was so scary."

"Now just hold on," said Grandpa. "I seem to recall that before Mr. Baker left for Europe he said some friends of his son might be camping on his place for a while. Are you sure you didn't just see some peo-

ple and then let your imaginations run
away with you?"

"No, Grandpa, no!" said Liza. "There
was a tepee and everything. Oh, Grandpa,

you've got to believe us! You've just got to!"

"Grandpa," said Bill, "why don't you go and see for yourself?"

"No," said Gran. "Nobody is going anyplace until you children calm down. Later on this afternoon, if you still want him to, your Grandpa will go and take a look."

"But, Gran!" said Liza.

"No buts about it," said Gran. "Here, Jed, you and Bill shell these peas. Liza, please dice these potatoes for salad."

In a few minutes Gran had all three children seated at the table working.

"Gosh," whispered Liza. "They really don't believe us."

"It does sound like a pretty wild tale," said Jed.

"But it is true!" said Bill. "We did see all that, didn't we?"

"We did," said Jed. "But you know, it's beginning not to seem real to me either."

18.

Surprises All Around

The children were sure they could not eat a bite, but to their surprise, when lunch was ready, they found themselves very hungry.

As soon as they got up from the table Bill said, "Will you go now, Grandpa?"

"Be patient," said Grandpa. "There are a few dishes to be done first."

"Oh, phooey!" said Bill.

As Liza was washing she whispered, "Grown-ups are so impossible."

"They sure are," Bill whispered back. "But there's nothing we can do about it."

"We can get these dishes finished," said Jed.

"Yeah," said Bill. "And I'll bet they think of something else for us to do after that."

But when the dishes were done, Grandpa said, "All right, children, lead the way."

Liza hung back. She had decided to stay with Gran. But to everybody's surprise, Gran took off her apron and said, "I think I'll go with you. It's a nice day for a walk."

That decided Liza. She surely wasn't going to stay alone.

As they walked through the woods Gran said, "My, it's been ages since I've done this."

She and Grandpa chatted about various trees and bushes they saw. The children walked a little ahead.

"Listen to that, will you?" said Bill. "You would think we were just taking a nature walk!"

"As far as they're concerned, we are,"

said Jed. "They still think we just imagined all this."

"Well, they'll soon find out," said Liza. They had come to the edge of the woods, and the children waited behind the berry bushes for their grandparents.

Grandpa was ready to start right across the pasture. Bill said, "Hey, Grandpa! Don't you think we should try to stay low and out of sight?"

"Oh, I don't think we'll run into any trouble," said Grandpa.

"Well, maybe we should at least use your handkerchief and make a white flag," said Jed.

Grandpa chuckled and said, "I declare! You children! What will you think of next?"

The children said no more, but their fingers were crossed the whole way across the pasture.

When they got to the other side, the

children were almost afraid to look. But not Grandpa! He marched right over to the edge of the hill. They all heard him exclaim, "Now that is a real sight. Hurry, Gran!"

"I'm coming, I'm coming," said Gran as she joined Grandpa. Then she exclaimed, "Why it does look like a real Indian camp!"

"Okay," said Bill, "don't you think we better go back now?"

"Go back!" said Grandpa. "We just got here. I want a closer look at those things."

"But, Grandpa . . ." started Liza and got no further for Grandpa was calling, "Hello there, anybody home?"

He called again, but there was no answer.

"Well," he said, "I don't think they will mind if we look around. Come this way, Gran. It's not quite as steep."

Without a word the children scampered

down the hill after their grandparents.

Liza still felt jumpy. She said, "Oh, please, Grandpa, let's go back."

But just as she said that they heard someone call, "Hey, Mom! Pop! Hurry, we've got company."

And out of the woods came a boy and girl with a cocker spaniel following close at their heels. Not far behind them came a man and woman.

Liza, Bill, and Jed just stared. These couldn't be the same people they had seen this morning. Their faces weren't painted, and they were dressed in ordinary clothes. The children did not know what to think now. Could it really have been their imaginations?

"Gee," said the boy. "We were getting ready to come and see you."

"Come see us!" said Liza.

"To apologize," said the girl. "Mom got awfully mad with us when we told her about taking the scraps."

"You mean you're the garbage thieves?" said Bill.

The two children looked surprised. The boy said, "But your note said you knew who we were."

Jed, Bill, and Liza looked quickly at each other. Jed said, "Our mistake."

Liza caught a glimpse of something red. Before anybody could question the note, she quickly said, "But what's my red sweater doing here?"

"What red sweater?" asked the boy.

"This one," said Liza as she pulled the sweater out from under a bush.

"Is that rag your sweater?" said the boy. "Our dog picked that up in the woods."

"Dog!" said Liza. "You mean you didn't leave it on a bush?"

The boy looked puzzled.

"You see," said Jed, "we found the sweater on a bush. We thought you needed it. We left you another note and some sandwiches on the same bush."

"Golly, this is a mixup," said the girl. "That crazy dog must have taken the sweater. He has a thing about anything wool. And we never knew anything about sandwiches."

"Phooey," said Bill. "I knew I should have eaten those sandwiches."

"Oh!" said the man. "Between our children and our dog, I think we have some explaining to do. First, I'm Bob Jackson. This is my wife, Linda, and our children, Mark and Alison."

Grandpa introduced himself and his family.

"Mr. Baker's son and I teach in the same college," began Mr. Jackson. "Besides teaching, I've been collecting material for a book on Indian culture. My whole family has been helping me. The more we found out, the more interested we became in their old way of life. So we decided for our vacation this year to camp out and try living Indian style."

"And after we got here we found out about our dog, Piper," said Alison.

"What about him?" asked Liza.

"Oh, he's the silliest dog!" said Alison. "We've been finding our own food, you know, plants and berries and stuff. For meat, we've been having mostly fish that we catch. But that dog won't eat any of it. He won't even eat fish. We tried giving it to him cooked and raw. All he would do was sniff at it and walk away. Pop said not to worry, Piper would eat when he got hungry enough. But Mark and I worried anyway."

"We even made some traps thinking we might catch something he would like," said Mark. "But so far we haven't caught a thing."

Jed laughed and said, "Yes, you did! You caught Jelly Bean."

"Jelly Bean!" said Alison. "Is that your puppy? Oh, he didn't get hurt, did he?"

"No, he's okay," said Jed.

"He must have followed us," said Mark. "You see Piper was the one who started taking the scraps. Early one morning Alison and I went exploring. We went through those woods across the pasture and ended up at your place. Piper ran over to your garbage can and that bag of scraps was on top. He took the bag before we could stop him and ran off into the woods. We were worried because we didn't know it was scraps. By the time we got to him he had torn the bag open and was eating. Then we saw it was only scraps. It seemed like the perfect answer to our problem. So after that we took the scraps every morning."

"But gee," said Alison. "We never thought about it as stealing. We would have asked, but nobody was up that early at your house."

"We just told Mom and Pop today. Mom wanted to send us right back to apologize," said Mark, "but Pop thought you might like some fresh fish. We caught some this afternoon to bring to you."

"Well," said Grandpa, "your father is right. I do love fresh fish, and I haven't had any lately."

"Oh," said Alison. "Why didn't you come sooner? We had such fun this morning."

"Yeah," said Mark. "We had a real pow-wow with costumes and war paint and all. You should have been here."

Grandpa chuckled loudly. Even Gran had to smile as Grandpa said, "Oh, they were here."

"You were!" said Alison. "Then why didn't you join us?"

"Well," said Jed, "it was like this. You folks didn't look very friendly this morning."

"In fact," said Bill, "you scared us to pieces."

By the time they finished telling their adventure, Liza, Bill, and Jed were laughing with the others.

19.

Mud Pie Fish

"I have an idea," said Mr. Jackson. "Instead of taking the fish home with you, why don't you folks stay and we'll cook them in an Indian way for you."

"Oh, Gran, Grandpa!" said Liza, "Do say yes."

"Of course we'll say yes," said Grandpa. "We would be delighted to stay."

"Yipee!" said Mark. "We'll get the clay, Pop."

"Clay!" said Liza. "For what?"

"You'll see," said Mark. "Come with me and help."

Mark picked up a bucket and the other children followed him. Mr. Jackson called, "Mark, on your way back pick up the fish, please."

"Okay, Pop," Mark called back.

The children walked along the bank of the stream.

"Here," said Mark. "This is the best clay. So dig in."

They used sticks to help them dig into the clay bank.

"Gosh, this sure is sticky stuff," said Bill.

"Is it the same kind the Indians used to make pottery?" asked Liza.

"Yes," said Alison. "Mom and I are trying to make some ourselves."

Soon the children had half filled the bucket.

"That's enough," said Mark. "Now for the really gooky part."

Mark cupped his hands and dipped some water from the stream. He put several handfuls in with the clay and began

to mix it into a smooth, thick paste.

"I sure don't know what this is all about," said Bill. "But I guess it's all right."

Alison laughed and said, "You'll understand soon."

"Now for the fish," said Mark. "You two fellows carry this bucket, and I'll get them."

Liza followed Mark.

"They should be right around here," he said. "Oh, there's the basket."

Liza saw a basket almost submerged in the water.

"But if you have already caught them, why do you have them in the water?" she asked.

"To keep them from spoiling," said Mark. "We don't have an icebox and meat spoils quickly. The stream water is cold enough to keep them fresh."

"Gee," said Liza. "That's a neat idea."

The children carried the clay and fish back to the camp. As soon as Grandpa saw them coming he said, "Now that is a nice lot of fish!"

"Bring them here, Mark," said Mr. Jackson. "Let's get them ready to cook."

Mr. Jackson took a knife and slit along the bottom of each fish. Then he cleaned out the insides.

"We can help you scale them," said Jed.

"Oh, we don't scale them," said Mark.

"Ugh!" said Liza. "Are we supposed to ⸮t the scales?"

147

"Oh, no," said Alison. "You see we wrap each fish in clay and bake it in the fire. The skin sticks to the clay. When we take the clay off, the skin and scales come off with it."

"Now I never heard of that," said Gran.

"Okay, they're all yours," said Mr. Jackson as he finished cleaning out the last fish.

"Now do we cover them?" asked Jed.

"Yes," said Mark. He picked up a fish and completely covered it with clay.

"Gosh, these fish are slippery," said Liza as she tried to pick one up.

"This takes me back to my mud pie days," said Bill.

With all of the children working, the job was soon finished. A row of clay packages, each containing a fish, lay before them.

"Okay, Pop, all through," said Alison.

"Fine," said Mr. Jackson. "Now you all

scurry around and gather loads of twigs and some small wood."

"Wait a minute," said Mrs. Jackson. "We will want some bread with the fish. I need the girls to pound the corn."

"Pound the corn!" said Liza.

"Oh, yes," said Alison. "You have to work to get bread around here. Come on, I'll show you."

Alison led Liza over to a hollowed log with a smaller log standing in it.

"Is that what we use?" asked Liza.

"Yes," said Alison. "It's a mortar and pestle. You dump corn into the mortar and pound with the pestle."

As Alison talked, she poured some corn into the hollowed-out log.

"Okay," she said. "You get on the other side. It's easier if we pound together."

The girls moved the pestle up and down, with each pound crushing the corn into finer pieces.

"This is hard work," said Liza. "But it's kind of fun, too."

By the time the girls had finished pounding and sifting the corn meal, the boys had collected a great pile of twigs and small pieces of wood. Mr. Jackson made a fire and put the clay-covered fish in it. Then he put more wood on top of the fish.

"There," he said. "If we keep the fire hot enough it shouldn't take too long for those to cook."

In the meantime Mrs. Jackson added salt and water to the corn meal and mixed it into a thin batter.

"And when the fish are cooked," she said, "it will only take a few minutes to do the bread."

Later Mr. Jackson poked the clay-covered fish with a stick and declared them ready. He raked them out of the fire.

"I'll get the water," said Mark.

"We're always too hungry to wait for

the clay to cool," explained Alison, "so we pour water over it."

While the children cooled the clay with stream water, Mrs. Jackson cooked thin crispy cakes of corn bread.

"I think everything's ready," said Mr. Jackson. "We've found the best way to eat this fish is to crack the clay on one side and peel it off. Then we use a piece of bread to dig the fish meat out. The clay on the other side makes a bowl."

Liza looked doubtful as she picked up a fish. But when she cracked the clay and peeled it off, steamy white fish meat appeared.

"Ummm, that does look good," she said. She took a piece of bread and dug out a chunk of meat.

"And it tastes just as good," she said.

Soon everybody was so busily eating the fish and crispy bread there was no time for talk. It was only when the last fish and last bread had been eaten that Grandpa said,

"Now I declare, those Indians really did know how to cook fish!"

"I'm with you there," said Bill.

"But my goodness," said Gran, "look at how late it is. This has been so pleasant I don't know where the time went. We really must be going."

While the grownups said their good-byes, the children made plans for the next day. Soon Gran, Grandpa, Liza, Jed, and Bill were on their way across the pasture.

"Well, Gran," said Jed, "I guess that solves your mystery."

"And boy, the solution was sure a surprise," said Bill.

"Yes," said Liza. "Here all this time we thought we were feeding children, and it turns out to be a silly dog."

"What?" said Grandpa. "What on earth are you talking about?"

Then the children told Gran and Grandpa the whole story.

Grandpa shook his head and said, "You

children! The things you do keep to yourselves!"

By this time they were nearing the house.

"Hey, who left all the lights on?" asked Jed.

The house was ablaze with light. Everybody was puzzled.

"Well," said Grandpa, "it seems as if we have another mystery for you children to solve."

"Oh, no!" groaned Bill. "I've had enough mystery for a while."

Just as he said that, the back door opened. A man and woman stepped out.

"Mom! Dad!" shouted Liza.

And with wild whoops the three children raced to the house.